Spooky Night

by Natalie Savage Carlson

illustrated by Andrew Glass

Lothrop, Lee & Shepard Books
New York

Library of Congress Cataloging in Publica-
tion Data. Carlson, Natalie Savage. Spooky
night. Summary: A witch's black cat who
wishes to become a family pet must perform
one last bit of magic before he can be free.
[1. Cats—Fiction. 2. Witches—Fiction.
3. Halloween—Fiction] I. Glass, Andrew,
ill. II. Title.
PZ7.C2167Sp   [E]   82-54
ISBN 0-688-00934-4   AACR2
ISBN 0-688-00935-2 (lib. bdg.)

For Meaghan Mahoney,
the daughter of my friends
Tucky and Jimmy

One night when the wind screeched and the moon was full, Mrs. Bascomb came home from a PTA meeting. She saw a black cat sitting on the welcome mat.

"What are you doing here, kitty?" she asked. "Don't you have a home somewhere?"

The cat only stared at her with his eyes getting greener and greener. His whiskers twitched and his black tail switched.

Then he rubbed against her jeans and purred. Mrs. Bascomb opened the door and the cat followed her in, pussyfoot, pussyfoot to the kitchen.

The Bascomb girl and boy were there, studying their lessons at the table. They were surprised to see a strange cat with their mother.

"Where did you find him?" asked the Bascomb girl.

"I didn't find him," said Mrs. Bascomb. "He found us."

"I've never seen him around here," said the Bascomb boy.

"He looks like a witch's cat," said the Bascomb girl. "Let's keep him and call him Spooky."

The cat only stared at them with his eyes getting greener and greener. His whiskers twitched and his tail switched.

Then he jumped up on an empty kitchen chair. He lay down with his tail hanging over the side. He closed his eyes and purred himself to sleep.

So that is the way Spooky became the Bascombs' pet.

He turned out to be a proper cat even if he had arrived when the wind screeched and the moon was full.

He was a quiet cat. He was a gentle cat.

He was an affectionate cat.

He liked to lie on a Bascomb lap and purr.

It wasn't until the last day of October that Spooky began acting strangely.

He sat in the middle of the floor and howled and yowled and squalled as if Something was standing on his tail.

He jumped into the air and rolled over and over as if Something was trying to grab him.

He climbed up the curtain and jumped on top of the bookcase as if Something was after him.

The Bascomb girl
said, "I've never seen
him act like this."

The Bascomb boy
said, "He seems to see
something we don't."

Mrs. Bascomb said, "Perhaps he wants to go out."

She opened the door. But Spooky crawled under the
bookcase as if Something was at the door waiting for him.

The Bascomb girl said, "I'm sure he belonged to a witch
and she is trying to get him back."

That night the young Bascombs put on their costumes to play trick or treat. The Bascomb boy was dressed like a ghost. All he needed was an old sheet with two holes for eyes. The Bascomb girl was dressed like a witch. She wore a tall black hat and a long black cape and a horrible mask.

When Spooky saw her, he crawled under the bookcase again. He looked at her with his eyes getting greener and greener. His whiskers twitched and his tail switched.

"Come with me, kitty," said the Bascomb girl. "You will be just right with my costume."

She reached under the bookcase to pull him out.

"*Pfft! Pfft!*" Spooky spat at her.

The Bascomb boy said, "He never did that before."

The Bascomb girl said, "Weird things happen on Halloween."

When they left, Spooky crawled out from under the bookcase. He went pussyfoot, pussyfoot to the kitchen.

Lying on a chair, with his tail hanging over the side, he purred himself to sleep. Not a whisker twitched, even when Mr. Bascomb opened the window a big crack for air.

Later the young Bascombs came home with bagfuls of candy and chewing gum and apples and some pennies from a woman who hadn't expected trick or treaters.

They ate some candy, then went to bed.

The lights went out. All was dark and quiet. Dong, dong, dong, and more dongs! The kitchen clock struck midnight. Spooky jumped up with a yowl as if Something had yanked his tail.

He jumped down from the chair. He went pussyfoot, pussyfoot across the floor. He jumped up on the sink and squeezed through the big crack of the window.

Outside, the wind screeched and the moon was full. It was like the night that Spooky had been found on the Bascombs' welcome mat.

He went pussyfoot, pussyfoot down the street. Every now and then he spat "*pfft, pfft*" at Something behind him.

He went pussyfoot, pussyfoot into the woods where branches scraped together like skeletons shaking hands.

A bent figure stepped from behind a tree. It looked like the Bascomb girl in her costume. It wore a tall black hat and a long black cape and had a horrible face. It was a real witch.

"I sent Something to bring you back to me," she said.

"*Pfft! Pfft!*" Spooky spat at her.

His whiskers twitched and his tail switched.

The witch cackled with a sound like dry twigs snapping,
"You ran away because you wished to be a real house pet."

"*Pfft! Pfft!*" Spooky spat at her again.

The witch said, "I shall give you the chance to have your wish. I want to play with the moon tonight but the handle of my flying broom is broken. Catch the moon for me and I will set you free."

Then she disappeared in a blue flash, and there was nothing left of her but a smell like a popped firecracker.

Spooky looked up at the sky. He jumped and jumped, higher and higher, but he couldn't reach the moon.

He jumped onto the tallest tree in the woods. He climbed up, up to the tip-top. He stood on his hind legs and clawed at the sky. But he couldn't reach the moon.

He howled and yowled and squalled because he would have to stay with the witch and her Something.

There was a hole in the tree. There was an owl inside the hole. He heard Spooky and came out. The owl clacked his beak and spread his wings.

"Who-oo! Who-oo are you-oo!" he hooted.
Spooky jumped from branch to branch. The owl flew
from branch to branch. A branch broke and Spooky went
flying through the air too.

Then the screeching wind grew stronger and stronger. It whipped the tree-tops. It whirled Spooky in the air.

It blew him higher and higher until he reached the stars.
Then it swept away with a last wild scream.

Spooky stepped from star to star until he reached
the moon.
He jumped on the moon.
He sharpened his claws.
He spun the moon around and around under his paws.

He sat on the moon and grabbed pawfuls of stars. He
flung them down until the sky was full of shooting stars.

The moon sank lower and lower until it reached the
ground. They were back on the Bascombs' street.

EXTENSION

Spooky rolled the moon down the street into the woods.
The witch was waiting for him.

"So you caught the moon for me," she cackled as she grabbed it with her bony fingers.

"Meow! Meow!" bragged Spooky because a black cat could catch the moon on Halloween.

The witch sneered. She said, "You are free to stay with your stupid humans and be a house pet. SCAT!"

Spooky scatted out of the woods.

He went pussyfoot, pussyfoot down the street to the Bascomb house.

He crawled through the window. He went pussyfoot, pussyfoot to the kitchen chair. With his tail hanging over the side, he purred himself to sleep.